# It's Winter

by
Jimmy Pickering

smallfellow press
LOS ANGELES

# To Mom and Dad

Thank you for making my winters pure magic

**W**hen Sally and Sam look down below,
They're happy to see the ground covered with snow.

**T**he once-barren trees
Are now puffy and white.

The blanket of snow
Has arrived in the night.

The cold days are here
(Of that there's no doubt).

It's time to discover
**What Winter's about.**

The air they're inhaling
Is chilly and crisp,
And out of their mouths
Comes a curly white wisp.

Flat on their backs
In the soft winter snow,
They stretch arms and legs
As far as they'll go.

Looking silly and kooky,
They flap up and down,
Making little snow angels
On the powdery ground.

They visit their clubhouse
High up in a tree,

And to their surprise
Make a discovery.

There, under the roof,
Surrounded by snow,

Are icicles sparkling
In one pretty row.

Grabbing for snowflakes is always great fun.

'Specially ones you can catch with your tongue.

Most people think snowmen
Are such fun to make,
With top hat and carrot
And arms from a rake...
But their plans are bigger;
They want a lot more.

So they make their snowman
A huge
dinosaur.

Inside there's warm cocoa
All ready to sip.

Sally giggles at Sam
With his chocolaty lip.

Making gingerbread houses
Is no easy feat,

But they ARE fun to build
And more fun to eat.

Sally and Sam
Are happy to see

Pretty red birds
In a white snowy tree.

They're certainly one of the Season's delights.

*S*ledding downhill
Is a fast, easy ride,
But it sure makes their tummies
All tickly inside.

**A**fraid that their Dino
Might start feeling chilly,

They go back and dress him
And, boy, he looks silly!

Along with the Ev'ning
Come nighttime delights.
There's nothing as pretty
As holiday lights.

The colors are bright
And, oh, what a glow,
Twinkling like magic
Right there in the snow.

All warm by the fire,
With mem'ries of fun,

They cannot believe
The day's really done.

They're playing and giggling
And thinking of when

They'll wake in the morning
And start up again.

Published by
Smallfellow Press
A division of Tallfellow Press, Inc.
1180 S. Beverly Drive
Los Angeles, CA 90035

Type and Layout: Scott Allen


ISBN 1-931290-16-4

Printed in Italy
10 9 8 7 6 5 4 3 2



Tallfellow Press, Inc
Los Angeles